BRAVING OUR SAVINGS

Holland and London Learn to Invest!

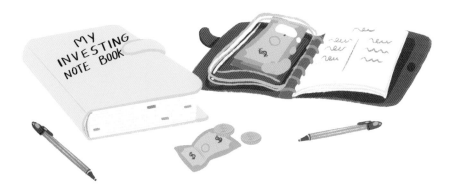

BY SARAH SAMUELS, CFA, CAIA

Published by Worth Books, an imprint of Forefront Books, Nashville, Tennessee.

Distributed by Simon & Schuster.

Library of Congress Control Number: 2023922120

Print ISBN: 978-1-63763-257-4
E-book ISBN: 978-1-63763-258-1

Cover Design and Illustrations by Sawyer Cloud
Interior Design by Mary Susan Oleson, Blu Design Concepts

MIX
Paper | Supporting
responsible forestry
FSC® C144853
FSC
www.fsc.org

*Be brave and
keep climbing,
little ones*

Holland

Nine-year-old Holland has a big idea. After she tells her six-year-old sister, London, about her plan, she calls her mom to the kitchen table for a family meeting.

"What if she says no?" whispers London while they wait.

"I'll never know if I don't ask her," Holland replies.

Mom comes into the kitchen and sits at the table. "Hey, girls! What's up?"

Holland takes a deep breath. "Mom, I think I'm old enough and responsible enough to get my ears pierced. I can pay for it with the money I've been saving."

"I'm impressed—you've really thought this through. Let me think about it," says their mom. "And let's see how much you have in your piggy bank."

When Holland counts her savings, her hope sinks like a stone in a river. She needs forty dollars to get her ears pierced, but she has only twenty-five dollars.

"I thought I had more in here," says Holland.

"There are a lot of ways to grow your money," her mother says. She shows the girls her own bank account **STATEMENT** and points to two things: the **BALANCE** and the **INTEREST** rate. "Interest is a reward for saving your money at the bank. If you keep your money in a piggy bank, it can't earn any interest."

"Another way to grow your money is to invest it," Mom continues.

"What's investing?" London asks.

"Investing is buying something with the hope it will increase in value and make money for you. Investing is risky, and sometimes you lose money," Mom explains.

"I want to invest!" says Holland.

"Me too!" London agrees.

"You can invest in something that pays **INTEREST**, like a savings account or a **BOND**. Or you could invest in the **STOCK MARKET**," Mom suggests. "Some **STOCKS** pay **DIVIDENDS**, which are kind of like interest."

"I'll teach you everything you need to know. Anyone can be an investor! I'll help you set up a **BROKERAGE ACCOUNT**, but first, you must do two important things."

Holland and London both lean in to listen.

"One, you have to research the stock you want to buy. And two, you have to brave your savings. Investors have to be brave," Mom says.

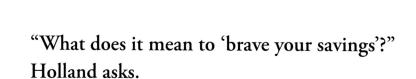

"What does it mean to 'brave your savings'?" Holland asks.

"When you brave your savings, you take a risk, do hard work like researching companies, and invest in things you believe in," Mom explains. "Why don't you go do your research, and then we'll take the next step?"

Excited, the girls go upstairs to London's bedroom,
and Holland makes a list of things she enjoys.

Next, she writes down companies related to what she enjoys.

Finally, with London's help, Holland creates a list of questions she can ask to figure out if the companies are good investments:

What does she love about the things they make?
What do other customers love about the company?
How long are the lines in the store?

After they finish, Holland and London go back down to the kitchen.

"Mom, we need a research trip to the mall," says Holland. "Can you please drive us there?"

"Sure! And while you're there, you can practice braving your savings."

At the mall, Mom gives Holland and London five dollars each for spending money.

First, they head to the makeup store. Holland notes what she sees: Lines are long. Customers look happy. Fresh Face could be a good stock to buy. Then Holland spies a glittery nail polish. It costs four dollars.

Should she buy the nail polish?
Or should she save her money to invest it?

Her best friend, Thiyoni, just bought this same nail polish. If her friends were there, she knows what they'd tell her to do: *Buy it!*

Holland picks up the nail polish and starts walking toward the cash register.

"What are you doing?" London asks her.

"Buying this nail polish. It's going to look great with my new dress."

"Holland, remember what Mom said: *'Brave your savings!'* If you buy that, you might not have enough money to buy stock and get your ears pierced."

Holland stops in her tracks. She sighs as she realizes her sister's right.

When she returns the nail polish to the shelf, she thinks,
It's really hard not to buy something I want right now!
But I need to keep my eye on the prize.

Holland is proud of herself—and now she'll have more money to invest!

After they get home, their mom opens **CUSTODIAL BROKERAGE ACCOUNTS** for each of them so they can buy stock.

London decides to buy one share of stock in her favorite sports gear company.

Holland will invest in two companies, Fresh Face and Brilliant Books, with her thirty dollars: the twenty-five dollars she already had in her account, plus the five dollars from Mom.

Wow, it's a good thing she didn't buy that nail polish! Because she saved that money, she can buy shares of stock in two companies instead of one. Investing in more than one company is smart because it provides **DIVERSIFICATION**. You can get diversification by buying different types of company's stocks or investing in an **INDEX FUND**.

"What if I make a mistake? I've never done this before!" says Holland.

"Thirty seconds of bravery, sis," says London. With a little help from Mom, Holland finds the **TICKER SYMBOL** for the company and completes her **TRADES**.

"I did it! I did research, bought stock, and braved my savings."

London jumps in the air and shouts,
"We're investors now!"

Holland watches the news and keeps track of what's happening with Fresh Face and Brilliant Books. She also checks the stock prices to see how they change over time. Before long, Holland's investment earns enough money for her to get her ears pierced.

When they hand her a mirror and she sees the sparkly gems in her ears, Holland smiles with pride. Her earrings feel like a badge of bravery.

On the way back to their house, London says, "I saw a cool necklace at the mall, the kind with a real shark tooth. Now that I know how to brave my savings, I'll be looking for my next stock to buy!"

AUTHOR'S NOTE TO KIDS

Did you know that you can be brave even when you're scared? Doing things that scare us is important in order for us to learn and grow. I call this "thirty seconds of bravery."

Practicing thirty seconds of bravery might mean doing something different than your friends, or being confident even though other people in the room don't look or act like you. By helping you make choices that move you toward your goals, practicing thirty seconds of bravery can help you become whoever you want to be!

AUTHOR'S NOTE TO PARENTS

Investing is exciting and interesting, and anyone can do it! The power of capital is tremendous. It keeps businesses functioning and funds innovation that can change the world—and it's an essential tool for people to lead healthy lives and retire comfortably. Capital is required for everyone to have access to education, for hospital systems to care for the sick, for climate change initiatives to succeed, and for social impact—equal access to opportunity, narrowing the wage gap, and other goals—to be achieved.

Careers in investing offer many wonderful opportunities. However, a very small percentage of capital is invested by women and people of color.* It's never too early to inspire young people of all backgrounds to invest.

This book is an introduction to some of the fundamental concepts of investing. Join me in teaching kids about this subject—and beginning to set right the imbalances of power in the investment industry and beyond.

*Source: Knight Foundation Diversity of Asset Management Report, 2021

INVESTING IN STOCKS

A share of a company, also called a **STOCK**, is a unit of ownership in that company. If you buy a share, you become an owner of this company, along with all the other stockholders in that company.

The same way that you grow each year, companies grow too—but not in height. A stock's earnings represent how much money the company makes. Companies want to grow earnings, so they can make money for you. Companies grow earnings by selling more of their products or by spending less money. Earnings can grow or shrink, and your money will grow or shrink with the company's earnings. Owners of stocks make money when the company does well and lose money if the company doesn't do well.

SOME STOCKS PAY DIVIDENDS, WHICH ARE REGULAR PAYMENTS BASED ON HOW MUCH MONEY THE COMPANY MAKES.

STOCKS CAN GO UP ⬆ AND DOWN ⬇

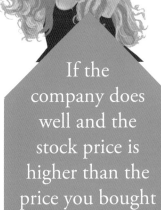

If the company does well and the stock price is higher than the price you bought it, you make money.

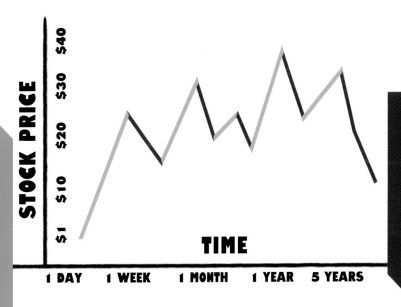

STOCK PRICE

$40
$30
$20
$10
$1

TIME

1 DAY   1 WEEK   1 MONTH   1 YEAR   5 YEARS

If the company does poorly and the stock price is lower than the price you bought it, you lose money.

STOCK RESEARCH WORKSHEET

Just like Holland and London researched their stocks before they invested, you can use this worksheet to research stocks! If a stock has more **X**s than ✔s, investing in that stock might be riskier. Think about whether you want to take that risk or invest in a stock with more ✔s.

	COMPANY INFO	✔ = GOOD X =NOT SO GOOD	NOTES
TICKER SYMBOL			
STOCK PRICE			
DIVIDEND			
EARNINGS GROWTH			
CUSTOMER INTERVIEWS			
HOW LONG ARE LINES AT THE COMPANY STORE?			
DO THEY HAVE A REWARDS PROGRAM?			
COOL THINGS THEY SELL OR SERVICES THEY OFFER			

TRADE DECISION: _____ BUY _____ DON'T BUY

READY TO INVEST? HERE'S HOW!

1. Open a custodial brokerage account with an adult's help
2. Enter your trade, based on your stock research worksheet

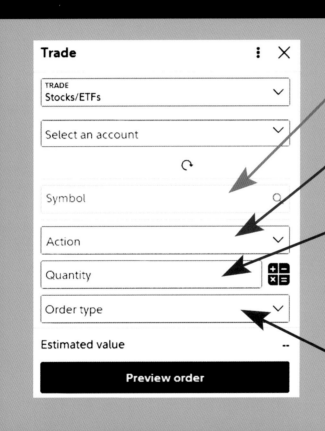

SYMBOL/TICKER:
This is a unique identifier for each company, or stock, you can buy on a stock exchange. Find the ticker online. You need to know the ticker in order to trade (Buy or Sell) the stock.

ACTION:
Buy or Sell

QUANTITY:
This is the number of shares you will trade. Calculate the cost of your trade by mulitplying the Quantity by the Stock Price. If you're buying, do you have enough money in your brokerage account for the purchase?

ORDER TYPE:
When you first start investing, Market Orders will work well. Market Orders trade the stock as soon as possible.

Trade ⋮ ✕

TRADE
Stocks/ETFs ⌄

Select an account ⌄

↻

Symbol 🔍

Action ⌄

Quantity

Order type ⌄

Estimated value --

Preview order

TALK LIKE A PRO!
A GLOSSARY OF INVESTING TERMS

Here are the definitions of some words investors use
so you can learn them and talk like a pro!

BALANCE: the amount of money in an account.

BOND: a type of investment in which a company borrows money from you and pays you interest while you wait to get your money back.

BROKERAGE ACCOUNT: an investment account that lets you buy and sell stock.

CUSTODIAL BROKERAGE ACCOUNT: a brokerage account your parents open for you because you are a kid. You're still the investor, though!

DIVERSIFICATION: a strategy of investing in many different stocks or bonds to reduce the risk of losing money. You can diversify by buying individual stocks and bonds that are different from one another, or you can buy an index fund.

DIVIDEND: a reward paid to you by some companies when you buy their stock. Dividend yield is paid as a percentage of the price of each share of stock and is one way you make money when you invest. (Yield = dividend / stock price. A higher dividend yield means higher payments.) Not all companies pay dividends, so pay attention to this when you're doing your stock research!

EARNINGS GROWTH: companies can grow by either selling more things or spending less money.

EQUITY: another word for a stock.

INDEX FUND: a single investment in hundreds of stocks at one time. One example is the S&P 500 Index, which invests you in five hundred different stocks.

INTEREST: a reward paid to you by a bank or company when you lend them your money. Interest can be paid monthly, quarterly, or annually. Make sure your bank is paying compound interest, which pays interest on both the money you save and the interest you earn. Compound interest is like magic and grows your money faster!

STATEMENT: a report that tells you how much money is in an account.

STOCK: a share of a company that is a unit of ownership in that company. If you buy a share of stock, you become a partial owner of this company (a stockholder). Stocks are also called equities.

STOCK MARKET: a place where people can buy and sell stocks.

TICKER SYMBOL: a unique abbreviation used to identify each public company. Kind of like your initials!

TRADE: the process of buying or selling a stock.